FOR THE MAL PAS BEACH CLEAN UP CREW.

WHAT ARE WE DOING?

LEAVING THIS BEACH A GOOD REVIEW.

First published 2022 by Walker Books Ltd, 87 Vauxhall Walk, London SE11 5HJ • 10 9 8 7 6 5 4 3 2 1 © 2022 Olaf Falafel • The right of Olaf Falafel to be identified as author/illustrator of this work has been asserted by him in accordance with the Copyright, Designs and Patents Act 1988 • This book has been typeset in Clarendon T Medium • Printed in China • All rights reserved. No part of this book may be reproduced, transmitted or stored in an information retrieval system in any form or by any means, graphic, electronic or mechanical, including photocopying, taping and recording, without prior written permission from the publisher. • British Library Cataloguing in Publication Data: a catalogue record for this book is available from the British Library • ISBN 978-1-4063-9765-9 • www.walker.co.uk

Blobfish

by Olaf Falafel

WALKER BOOKS

AND SUBSIDIARIES

LONDON • BOSTON • SYDNEY • AUCKLAND

It was an ordinary day by the sea.

People were splashing,

people were walking,

people were chasing

and people were whistling.

But under the sea ...

deep,
deep,
deep,
deep
under
the
sea ...

lived Blobfish.

Blobfish was all alone.

When Blobfish felt lonely, he told himself jokes.

KNOCK, KNOCK!
WHO'S THERE?
BLOBFISH
BLOBFISH WHO?
NO, IT'S ME, BLOBFISH!
NO, IT'S ME, BLOBFISH WHO?
NO, IT'S ME, BLOBF– OH FORGET IT, THIS IS USELESS.

Everywhere Blobfish looked,

other animals had friends to play with,

but Blobfish had no one.

So, Blobfish started to swim.

And while Blobfish was swimming,

people were talking,

people were cleaning,

people were playing

and people were eating.

And while Blobfish
was crying,

the bag
was flying,

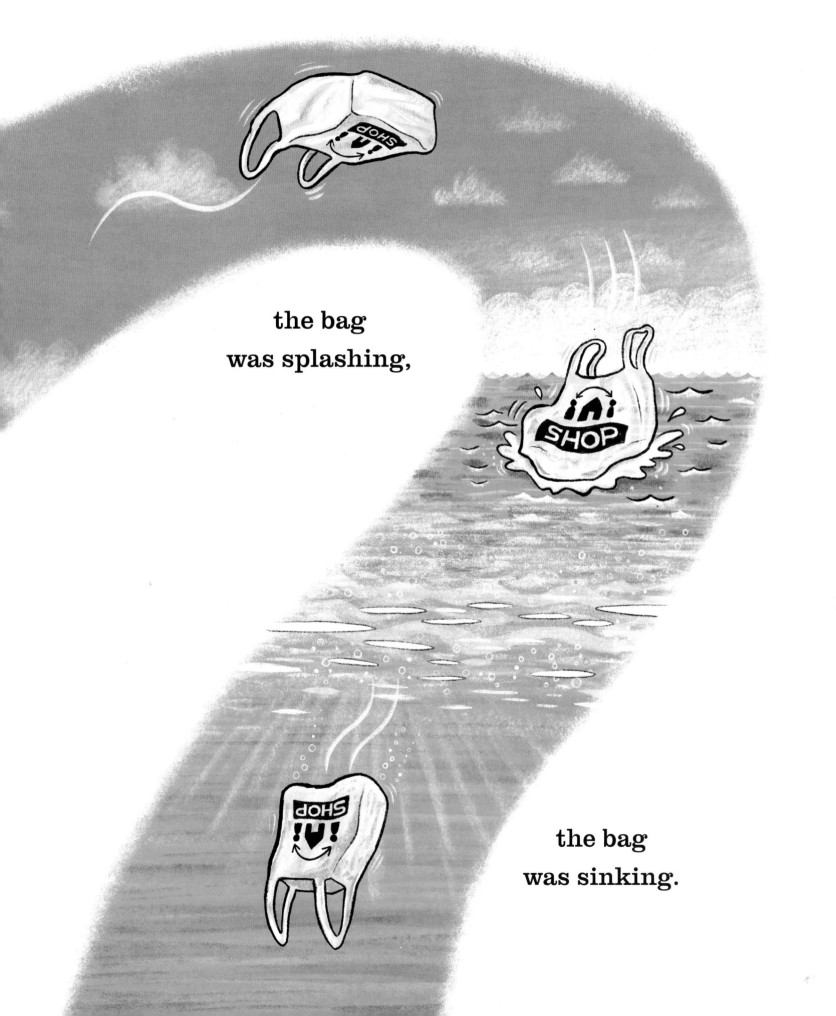

the bag
was splashing,

the bag
was sinking.

Then, out of the
corner of his blobby eye,
Blobfish spotted...

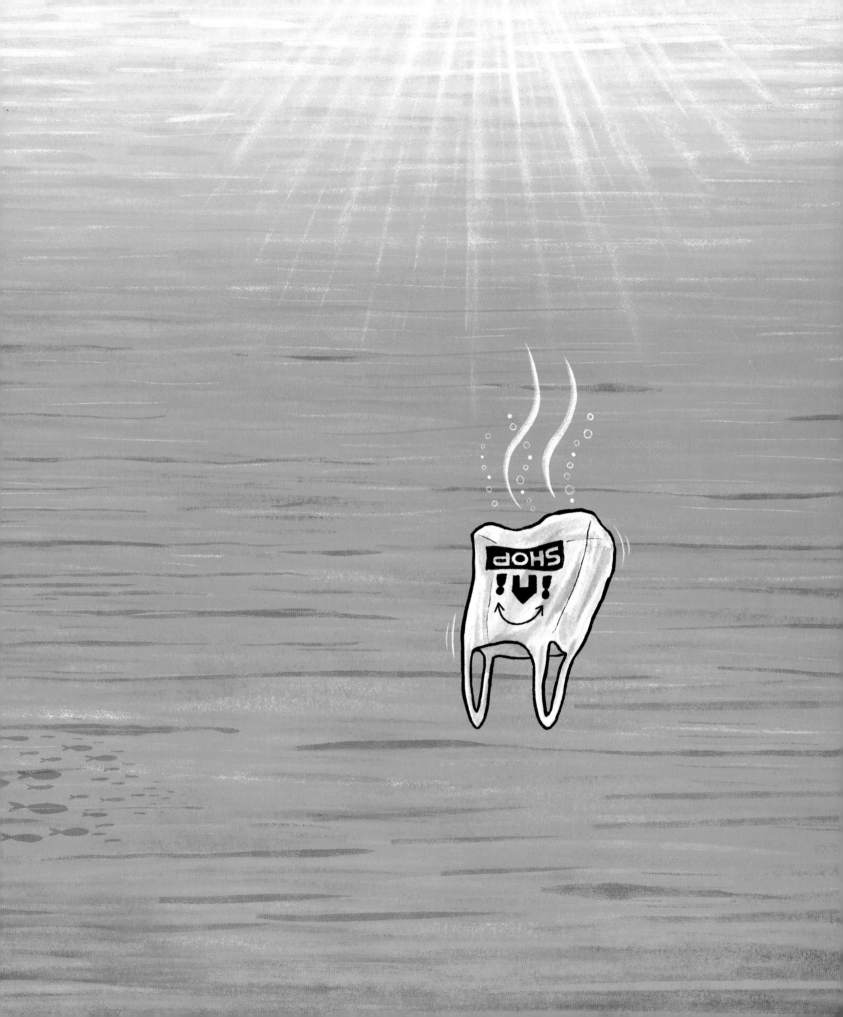

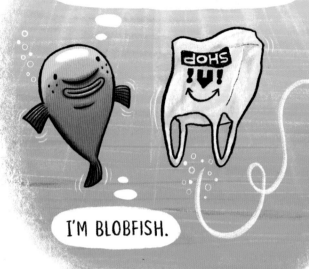

But just when it seemed like it could be too late...

A claw grabbed the bag and Blobfish fell out.

Blobfish
was
in
BIG
trouble!

A pinch and a sneeze and Blobfish was back.

And they lived

blobbily ever after!